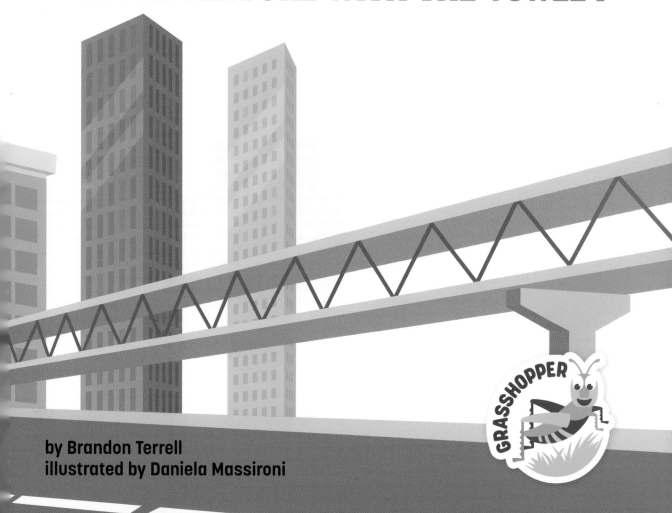

VOWEL ADVENTURES

IVAN IN THE CITY
AN ADVENTURE WITH THE VOWEL I

by Brandon Terrell
illustrated by Daniela Massironi

GRASSHOPPER

Tools for Parents & Teachers

Grasshopper Books enhance imagination and introduce the earliest readers to fiction with fun storylines and illustrations. The easy-to-read text supports early reading experiences with repetitive sentence patterns and sight words.

Before Reading

- Look at the cover illustration. What do readers see? What do they think the book will be about?

- Look at the picture glossary together. Sound out the words. Ask readers to identify the first letter of each vocabulary word.

Read the Book

- "Walk" through the book, reading to or along with the reader. Point to the illustrations as you read.

After Reading

- Review the picture glossary again. Ask readers to locate the words in the text.

- Ask the reader: What does a short 'i' sound like? What does a long 'i' sound like? Which words did you see in the book with these sounds? What other words do you know that have these sounds?

Grasshopper Books are published by Jump!
5357 Penn Avenue South
Minneapolis, MN 55419
www.jumplibrary.com

Library of Congress Cataloging-in-Publication Data

Names: Terrell, Brandon, 1978-2021 author.
Massironi, Daniela, illustrator.
Title: Ivan in the city: an adventure with the vowel i by Brandon Terrell; illustrated by Daniela Massironi.
Description: Minneapolis, MN: Jump!, Inc., [2022]
Series: Vowel adventures
Includes reading tips and supplementary back matter.
Audience: Ages 5-7.
Identifiers: LCCN 2021000215 (print)
LCCN 2021000216 (ebook)
ISBN 9781636902432 (hardcover)
ISBN 9781636902449 (paperback)
ISBN 9781636902456 (ebook)
Subjects: LCSH: Readers (Primary)
City and town life–Juvenile fiction.
Classification: LCC PE1119.2 .T475 2022 (print)
LCC PE1119.2 (ebook)
DDC 428.6/2–dc23
LC record available at https://lccn.loc.gov/2021000215
LC ebook record available at https://lccn.loc.gov/2021000216

Editor: Eliza Leahy
Direction and Layout: Anna Peterson
Illustrator: Daniela Massironi

Printed in the United States of America at Corporate Graphics in North Mankato, Minnesota.

Brandon M. Terrell (B.1978-D.2021) was a talented storyteller, authoring more than 100 books for children. He was a passionate reader, Star Wars enthusiast, amazing father, and devoted husband. This book is dedicated in his memory. Happy reading!

Table of Contents

City Sights

Ivan likes living in the city.

"I'm going to pick up dinner," Ivan's big sister, Ivy, says.

"I will come with!" says Ivan.

They stride along the sidewalk.

A fire engine flies by.

"Yikes!" Ivan cries.

Birds sing. *Chirp!*

Phones ring. *Ring!*

Clocks chime. *Ding!*

"I spy the deli!" Ivan says.

Ivan and Ivy pick up a pizza.
It is big!

10

"Let's sit in the sunshine," Ivy says.

Ivy and Ivan quickly finish the pizza.

11

In an instant, it is nighttime.

Ding! Ring! Chirp!

The city isn't tired.
But Ivan is!

Ivan and Ivy go inside.

"I'm wiped," Ivan says.

Ivan slides open
his window.

Ivan smiles. "Good
night, city!"

Let's Review Vowel I!

Point to the words with the short 'i' sound you saw in the book.
Point to the words with the long 'i' sound.

ring   **instant**   **smiles**   **big**   **likes**   **tired**

Picture Glossary

chime
To make a ringing sound, like a bell or a clock.

deli
A store that sells prepared foods.

fire engine
A large truck that carries pumps, hoses, ladders, and firefighters to a fire.

stride
To take long, energetic steps.